A.K. Johnston:
To Laurie, Lindsey, Luke and Ian – who first loved Onslo
And to the Father – who never stops looking.

Kristen & Kevin Howdeshell:
to our newest Marganser, Margo Baby,
and our bigs who are learning to read themse...
Emerson & Vera.

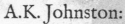

Published by Sleeping Bear Media - Kansas City
To contact author, ordering information and group sales visit: Onslobook.com
To contact the Howdeshells visit: thebraveunion.com

ONSLO

By A.K. Johnston

Illustrations by Kristen & Kevin Howdeshell

1. The Club

It wasn't much of a clubhouse, just the underside of a tall evergreen tree, but it was big enough to cover the seven young geese gathered under it.

It wasn't even an official club, but Nick (being the loudest) called himself "Top-Goose" and made the others start each meeting by

repeating the club "rules":

"All right," Nick honked,
"You all know the rules.
Let's hear 'em!"

"nn .. Yeh!" said Norman.
("nn .. Yeh" was Norman's way of saying
"Yes" - which he always said whenever
Nick spoke).

On Nick's cue all the geese, except one,
squawked:

"Geese don't talk to ducks!

Geese don't read - they fly!

And if you can get a free meal...

take it!"

2

Ha

With this they began laughing, falling all over themselves, and pointing at the one silent goose, named Onslo.

Ha Ha

Ha Ha Ha

Ha Ha Ha Ha Ha

Ha Ha Ha Ha Ha Ha Ha Ha Ha Ha

Ha Ha Ha Ha Ha Ha Ha Ha Ha

Ha

3

As the others laughed, Onslo wondered why he came to these silly meetings. He knew Nick's "rules" were written just to make fun of him.

Besides, Onslo wondered, what is so wrong with a goose that likes ducks? Onslo was friends with a family of mallards he met on the other side of the bay.

And so what if a goose can read? Onslo loved to read!

And, by golly, after hearing his dad's stories about lazy geese who live in huge, smelly flocks, on public ponds, eating nothing but handouts and getting so fat they can't fly, Onslo wasn't planning a life of free meals either.

No, Onslo didn't see a whole lot of sense in the club rules. He didn't much like Nick and Norman either. But the other geese were his friends, so Onslo endured their jokes. Besides, the rules weren't going to matter much longer. It was getting colder. Every free goose knows what cold weather means: migration- the "Big Flight" - time to fly south!

2. *Flight Training*

Onslo and his family lived near the bay of a big lake in Canada. It was a beautiful place, but it got too cold in the winter. The heavy snow would bury their food and the winter winds would freeze their lake solid. To survive the winter, they had to fly many, many miles south.

For Onslo and the other young geese, this would be their first "Big Flight." And, because they were young, it would be dangerous. They had to be trained. Onslo and his friends worked very hard to prepare. They practiced take-offs and landings, cold weather survival and, most importantly, flying in a "V" formation. They listened for hours as older geese described the route they would take and how to care for each other if something went wrong.

30...
31...

6

3. Reading

Each day after flight training, Onslo's friends usually went home to play checkers or to gossip under the evergreen. Onslo, however, would find a quiet place and do something different

- he would read.

Now, since I first mentioned it, you might be thinking: "Geese can't read!" And it's true, most geese can't read, or at least they can't anymore (someday I'll tell you that sad tale).

But Onslo could.

7

It was Onslo's mom and dad who taught him to read, first by arranging seeds or berries to spell out his name:

And then by spelling out other important words:

Soon Onslo knew most of the alphabet. He sometimes confused his 'i's and 'e's – like when he spelled "he" as "hi" and "me" as "mi" – but he kept at it and became a good reader.

But Nick and Norman kept making fun of him.
  "What does a goose need to read for?" snorted Nick.
  "nn .. Yeh," said Norman.
  "Geese fly, they don't read."
  "nn .. Yeh," echoed Norman.
Nick continued, "What good is reading when you're 15,000 feet in the air?"
  "nn .. Yeh," said Norman as they laughed trying to picture a goose with a book that high in the sky.

Sometimes, when his friends made jokes about his reading, Onslo would get discouraged and tell his mom he didn't want to read anymore.

She would nuzzle up to him and say "Don't worry, Onslo. One day, what you have learned will matter ... just keep at it!"

"But," he protested, "The club rules..."

"Oh, Onslo, what Nick or that club says doesn't matter. What matters is the truth. No club or rules can change what's true. You were made for a reason, and you are reading for a reason."

Onslo didn't always feel better, but he did a smart thing:

He trusted his mom and kept reading.

4. The Big Flight

The big day finally came. It was time to fly.

It was a cold morning. Snow was in the air even though the leaves had not all fallen. All the geese seemed nervous as they awaited the signal from the real "Top Goose" (not Nick) to begin.

As they waited, Onslo noticed that above them, the air was already full of hundreds of other geese from other flocks. They were migrating too! Onslo had never been this excited. It felt like his wing tips were buzzing.

With a signal from the Top Goose, Onslo's flock took off in a flurry of wings and loud honks. They were headed south.

They climbed higher and higher into the air. Onslo had never flown so high. The earth below looked strange and beautiful. He saw things as he'd never seen them before; the huge lake, the tall cliffs, the long rivers. He wondered who could make such awesome things.

The geese flew in a big "V" formation. Each goose took turns flying at the front of the "V" so the group could stay strong and fly farther. Even the young geese got to lead a little. Eagles and hawks are much stronger and faster, but geese can fly farther and higher because geese fly together.

Also, when geese fly as a flock, they have a plan to help each other. Each goose has two buddies who fly with him, and if one is hurt, the other two stay with him until he dies or gets well enough to fly again. The flock flew many miles.

As night came, the young geese were glad when the leaders found a place to land and rest. The flock had made it through the first day. As exhausted as he was, Onslo had trouble getting to sleep because he, Nick and Norman stayed up bragging to each other about how well they had flown.

After a while, tiredness won out and they all fell asleep.

5. Trouble

The next morning Onslo awoke early. He knew right away something was wrong - the sky was thick with clouds. The temperature had dropped and the older geese looked concerned. Onslo could hear the elders talking:

"I hope it doesn't snow," said one.

"Snow is not so bad," said another, "as long as we don't get ICE!"

ICE. That was THE enemy for a goose. It didn't happen very often, especially this early in the year. In fact, Onslo's dad had never experienced a "Big Flight" ice storm. But one older goose said, "Sometimes ice will fall as thick as rain, and hit as hard as rocks, and knock whole flocks right out of the sky."

No one wanted to think about that. Besides, if they could just get a few more days further south they would be all right. The elders decided the flock should fly on as quickly as possible.

The clouds grew thicker as they flew, forcing the flock to fly low all day. This became tiring, as flying low is much harder to do. Later in the day it began to get darker and colder - Onslo could barely feel his beak. The Top Goose knew of some ponds just a few hours away. If they could make it there they could rest for the night. They had no choice but to keep flying.

The wind grew stronger and was now blowing directly at them. The adult geese, including Onslo's mom and dad, positioned themselves near the front of the "V" and took turns flying lead to make it easier for the younger geese to keep up. As a result, Onslo, Norman and Nick wound up in the back of the formation. As it became darker and harder to see, they listened for each other's honks.

It got colder and the wind grew stronger. Soon it started to snow. Then, suddenly, the snow turned to ICE! The flock pushed on but the ice only got bigger and started to hurt Onslo as it hit his wings. He turned his head to see how Norman and Nick were doing behind him. Right then Onslo saw a huge hunk of ice hit one of Norman's wings, and then he saw Norman begin to FALL!

Nick and Onslo did just as they were taught. They stayed with Norman as he lost altitude and honked as loudly as they could. But in the strong wind no one could hear them. And, because it was so dark, no one could see them either. Norman did his best to glide down using his uninjured wing but he was falling fast, and the ice kept pounding him hard. Onslo flew directly under Norman, and Nick tried to fly under Onslo. But ice was hitting them all now and Nick was falling too. Onslo moved to fly beneath both geese. In all the wind, ice, noise and confusion none of them saw how low they were, nor did they see the

TREES.

WHAM!

They crashed into a stand of pines and fell to the icy ground with a thud.
As the wind continued to howl, none of them moved.

6. Morning

The first thing Onslo noticed was the pine needles.
Someone had made a sort of nest surrounding him with
sticks and pine needles. Where was he? What happened?

Onslo couldn't remember very much; just snow and ice and falling.
It was still cold, but now it was day and the sun was shining. Had he been dreaming?
Just then Onslo saw a pile of snow and pine needles next to him begin to move.

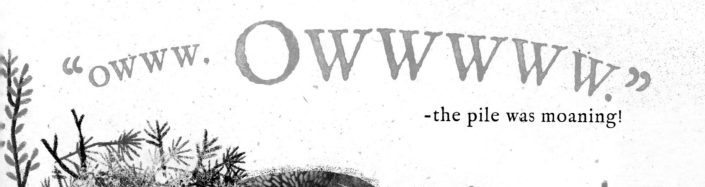

"owww. OWWWWW."

-the pile was moaning!

Onslo looked again... It was Norman! Someone had made a nest for him, too!
Onslo moved to help him. That's when the pain started. It felt like all of Onslo's
ribs were broken. When he tried to flap his wings, he couldn't - one wing was
broken. He hurt all over.

"nn. Where are we?" asked Norman, his voice barely a whisper from a nighttime

Hawk Nest
Beware!

Leg Lake

Best
duck
moss

They looked around. They were on the banks of a small, partially frozen lake. (You can see for yourself on the map.)

As they were looking around, some ducks paddled up to the bank.

"Well," said one duck, "Look who's up."

"Boy," the other said, "We thought you two might not make it!"

As Onlso started to reply, Norman whispered quickly, "Remember Onslo, geese don't talk to ducks!"

Onslo looked at Norman like his head was on fire. What an odd thing to say at a time like this. Onslo ignored Norman and asked the ducks, "Who are you?"

"We are the Mergansers," the male duck said. "Just call me Ganzer. And this is my wife, Merry."

"Are you the ones who rescued us from the storm and made those nests?" asked Onslo.

"Well, yes, but we had a lot of help from lots of other ducks."

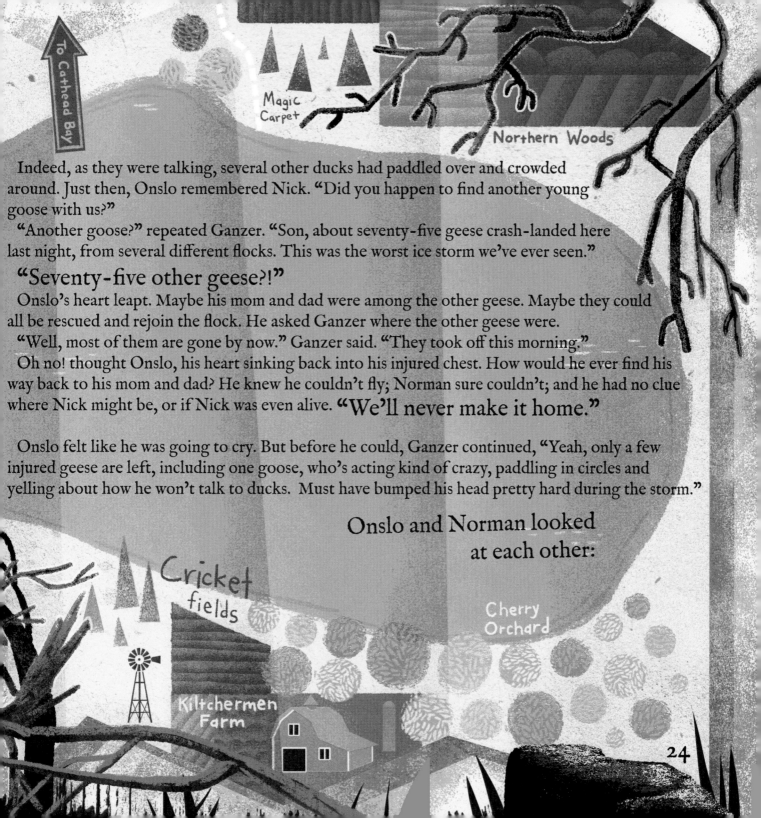

To Cathead Bay

Magic
Carpet

Northern Woods

Indeed, as they were talking, several other ducks had paddled over and crowded around. Just then, Onslo remembered Nick. "Did you happen to find another young goose with us?"

"Another goose?" repeated Ganzer. "Son, about seventy-five geese crash-landed here last night, from several different flocks. This was the worst ice storm we've ever seen."

"Seventy-five other geese?!"

Onslo's heart leapt. Maybe his mom and dad were among the other geese. Maybe they could all be rescued and rejoin the flock. He asked Ganzer where the other geese were.

"Well, most of them are gone by now." Ganzer said. "They took off this morning."

Oh no! thought Onslo, his heart sinking back into his injured chest. How would he ever find his way back to his mom and dad? He knew he couldn't fly; Norman sure couldn't; and he had no clue where Nick might be, or if Nick was even alive. **"We'll never make it home."**

Onslo felt like he was going to cry. But before he could, Ganzer continued, "Yeah, only a few injured geese are left, including one goose, who's acting kind of crazy, paddling in circles and yelling about how he won't talk to ducks. Must have bumped his head pretty hard during the storm."

Onslo and Norman looked
at each other:

Cricket
fields

Cherry
Orchard

Kiltchermen
Farm

24

"**Nick!**" Sure enough, as they spoke, another goose was being led across the lake. He was honking and protesting and carrying on. It was Nick.

"Boy, am I glad to see you two," confided Nick in a whisper to Onslo and Norman. "These ducks have been trying to wear me down all day, but I haven't given in. They'll get no goose secrets from me. I think they plan to make slaves of us ... They're mean ones, I can tell."

"nn.. You really think so?" asked Norman.

"Absolutely!" whispered Nick, "Check out how they're looking at us with their beady little duck eyes."

"nn .. Yeh!" he said slowly with growing suspicion, "Maybe you're right."

"Of course, I'm right. They're just acting nice now. But when we let our guard down, Wham! - they'll clip our wings and make slaves of us for sure. You don't want to spend the rest of your life catching minnows and pulling up duck moss for them, do you?"

"But Nick," Onslo said, "I think they saved our lives."

"Well, that's just like you, Onslo, to make nice with ducks. Maybe you should go read a book with them, too."

"nn .. Yeh!" said Norman, moving closer to Nick.

"Remember our rule," Nick continued: "'Don't talk to ducks' - ducks can't be trusted."

"nn .. Yeh!" said Norman.

Onslo looked at them for a moment and then said quietly, "We don't have much choice, do we?"

As the ducks were getting ready to leave they brought some duck moss and minnows for the gees to eat. Onslo spoke up: "Thank you for helping us."

"Happy to do it!" said Ganzer.

Merry added, "We're just thankful that you're not hurt worse. You boys look pretty beat up. If you want to be able to fly out of here any time soon you'll need all the rest and food you can get."

But fly where? thought Onslo. We're lost.

Nick looked sideways at the food the ducks had placed in front of him. He sure was hungry. He whispered to Onlso: "How do we know this stuff isn't poisoned slave serum? You won't catch me eating it."

Nick continued, getting louder as he spoke: "Why are these ducks being so nice to us geese? Doesn't it make you suspicious?"

Ganzer overheard Nick's question, and he repeated it aloud as he thought about his answer. "Why are we ducks being nice to you geese? The way I see it, geese have feathers and ducks have feathers. That makes us related, doesn't it? So seeing that we're family, we didn't think you'd mind

Now you boys need to eat and rest - we'll be back later."

Onslo started to eat, but Nick and Norman held back.

"I'm hungry," Norman said to Nick: "I feel weak."

"It's slave serum, I'm tellin' ya -- don't eat it!" Nick snarled.

"Think of it as a free meal, Nick," Onslo said, chuckling a little at the thought of Nick breaking one of his own rules.

"Funny," muttered Nick, still not eating, and every once in a while glancing over to see what effect the "poison" might be having on Onslo.

28

7. The Report

Later, as he rested, Onslo thought about his family. He wondered how he and his friends would ever rejoin their flock. Surely his mom and dad would be searching for him. But how long would it take? Would it be days, weeks or months before they were rescued?

Onslo soon learned more - and it wasn't good. Ganzer was apparently some sort of high-ranking leader among the ducks in the area, because all that morning, ducks from different ponds and lakes flew in with reports for him.

Onslo overheard the reports, including one duck telling Ganzer: "This was the worst storm I've ever seen. There must be ten thousand geese, most of them young, scattered on ponds and lakes from here to Charlevoix. On Lake Leelanau alone, more geese are stranded than we can count. At this point there's no way we can find these little guys' parents, or anyone else in their flock for that matter."

So there it was - the bad news! They were stuck! How could Onslo's parents find him and his friends, with so many other geese stranded, and so many other lakes and ponds to search? Onslo and Norman were too injured to fly, and Nick, who still wouldn't eat duck food, was far too weak. And besides, where would they fly to? They were lost and in trouble.

That night Onslo told Nick and Norman about all the news he'd heard. "I'm scared," he said.

"You're a book-readin' baby," honked Nick.
"I'll figure something out."
"nn .. Yeh!" said Norman.

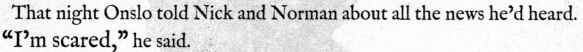

Nick continued: "I think that slave serum is starting to work on you Onslo."

"In fact, if you had spent more time learning to fly and less time rearranging seeds and berries and reading we wouldn't be in this mess!"

"nn .. Yeh!" said Norman
"Whadya mean?" Onslo protested.
"I mean if you'd been a better flyer you would've been able to keep Norman in the air when the ice hit his wing."

"nn .. Yeh!" said Norman slowly as if he wasn't so sure.
"But Nick," Onslo sputtered, "we might have made it
ntil you got clobbered so hard. You probably don't
emember it, but I had to leave Norman to fly under you."

"Well, who said you needed to do that? I don't need
any help from you or from these stupid ducks either!"
As Nick finished there was a strange silence ... Norman
wasn't speaking.

"Well, Norman?" demanded Nick, "Am I right?"
Norman remained silent.

"Aren't you gonna say, 'nn .. Yeh?'"

Finally Norman blurted out in tears,
"nnnnn.. No! You're wrong Nick. Onslo
isn't a book-readin' baby! He did try to help...the
ducks aren't gonna kill us and...
I'm hungry and ...
I want my mommy!!!"

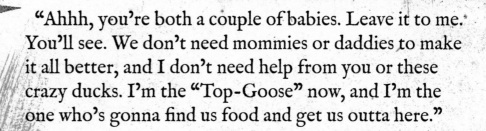

"Ahhh, you're both a couple of babies. Leave it to me.
You'll see. We don't need mommies or daddies to make
it all better, and I don't need help from you or these
crazy ducks. I'm the "Top-Goose" now, and I'm the
one who's gonna find us food and get us outta here."

At that point Norman, Onslo and Nick were too
tired to fight any more. It had been the longest day
of their lives. Soon they all fell asleep.

8. *His Father's Voice*

That night Onslo was awakened by a distant sound.
It was a sound he'd heard many times before.
It was his father's voice, honking far off in the night sky.

33

His dad was looking for him!

HONK!

Onslo tried to honk back but his young voice couldn't be heard above the snow covered pine trees. He tried to fly but he couldn't. He woke Nick and Norman. They honked too. Nick tried to fly but, because he hadn't eaten he was too weak and only got a few feet before crash-landing on his belly. Then, as quickly as they heard it, Onslo's fathers' honks faded in the distance. He was gone. It was too late.

34

9. A New Day

The next morning Onslo thought he heard his dad again, but this time when he looked up he saw the sky was full of geese from many different flocks, all honking and searching for their lost friends and family members. It slowly sank in. Onslo's flock would have to move on soon in order to get south before the next big storm.

Onslo began to realize that he and his friends would never get home.

Now even Nick started to worry. "We're in big trouble, Onslo. Your dad has finished his flyover. He had his chance to hear us but didn't. Now he probably won't be coming back."

Onslo agreed. It didn't look good.

Just then Ganzer paddled up. "Don't give up, boys!"

"Why not?" asked Onlso, "Our flock can't search for us forever. They have to move on without us."

"Look, just don't give up hope." Ganzer said.

"But why?" Onslo said slowly. "Do you know something we don't?"

"Well, yes and no," Ganzer said. I can't say for sure, and I don't expect you to understand it now, but fathers and mothers never stop looking for their children. A goose can get lost in an ice storm like you did, or he can get lost in a million other ways ... even after he's all grown up. But fathers and mothers never stop searching, never stop looking, no matter how hard it is or how long it takes."

"Do you mean my dad will come back and look again?" asked Onslo.

"If he's a father, he will," said Ganzer.

"Not everyone has a father, Ganzer," Nick muttered (not realizing that he was breaking his club rule by talking to a duck). "My dad disappeared a long time ago, long before our flock started flying south. So he's not up there lookin' for me. And even if he was, how could he, or Onslo's dad ever see us down here on just one of a thousand lakes and ponds?"

"Well," said Ganzer, "that is the bigger problem ... but there is a solution. Love finds a way ... a parent's love plants seeds that bloom when you need them."

"Seeds?" Onslo asked, "Seeds? Seeds! I've got it! Ganzer, do you have any seeds?"

"Seeds in snow? I suppose we could find a few, but not more than ten."

"Uuugh, that's not enough," cried Onslo.

"What do you need seeds for?" asked Nick

"You wouldn't understand Nick. It's something my mom and dad taught me. I need seeds or berries and lots of them!"

"Well, good luck with that," Nick sneered,
"all we got a lot of around here is ducks."
"nn .. Yeh!" sniffed Norman.

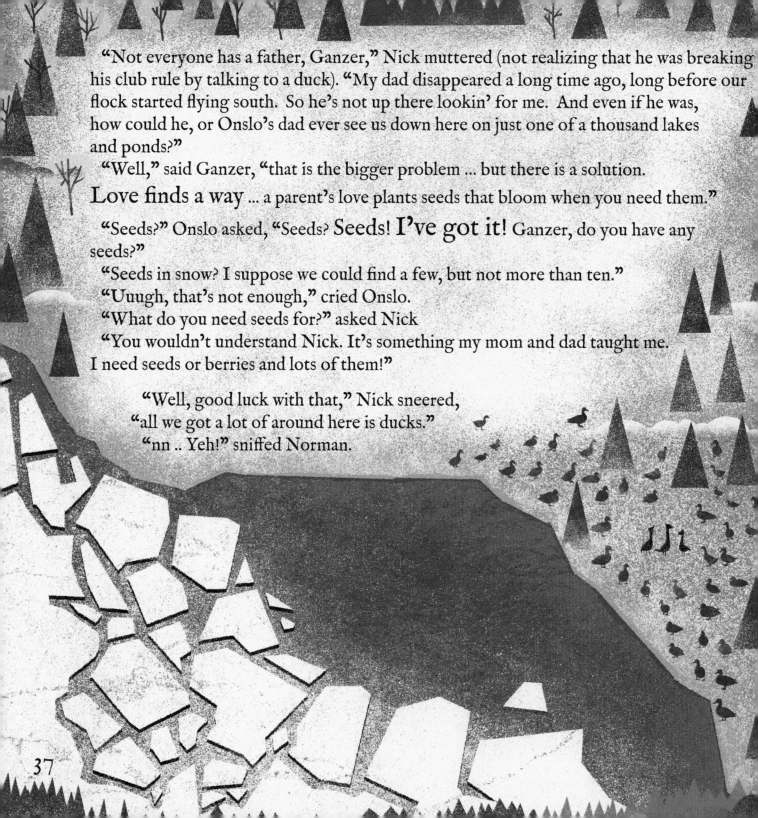

"In fact," said Nick, growing more agitated, "I've never seen so many lousy, stinkin', useless, rott..." And then, suddenly, Nick's voice and face brightened, as if he realized something "...lovely, lovely, beautiful DUCKS! Just look around you, Onslo - we got hundreds of lovely ducks!"

"Did Nick finally eat some duck moss?" asked Norman. "Are you all right?"

"I'm better than alright, little buddy, I'm reborn! Are you thinkin' what I'm thinkin', Onslo?"

"I think so," Onslo said slowly - "you mean use ducks instead of seeds?"

"nn .. Yeh!" Nick replied,"... I mean Yes!!"

"Oh no," whispered Norman, "they're both nuts on poisoned duck moss - we are gonna be slaves."

Onslo turned to Ganzer. "Ganzer, could you meet us in thirty minutes on the lake, in the middle of the frozen part, with as many ducks as you can find?"

"Only too happy to, but can you tell me why?"

"I can't," Onslo replied, "I have to go practice my spelling."

10. *The Gathering*

Thirty minutes later, Onslo, Nick and Norman met at the frozen part of the lake. Ganzer was already there with hundreds of other ducks -- mallards from Sutton's Bay and Leland, merganzers from as far as Mackinaw, wood ducks from Omena, Northport and Boyne City, and loons from Cathead Bay. There were even some swans from East Jordan and Glen Arbor. They all wanted to help and were curious about whatever these goofy geese were planning to do.

Onslo immediately took charge and, with Nick's help, began organizing and arranging the ducks on the ice, telling each of them exactly where to sit. He would sometimes stop and look down asking himself, "Now how many ducks in an 'o'?" Or he would say, "Is it 'i' or 'e'?" No one understood what he was doing except Nick, who was happily honking out Onslo's directions and quite comfortable bossing everyone around.

Finally, at about noon, Onslo was finished. "Now we just have to wait," he declared.

And they waited ... and waited.

Onslo asked Ganzer, "Did you really mean what you said about fathers?"
Ganzer replied, "Yes, Onslo, what I said about fathers and love is true, and it's also true for mothers. I believe your father is still searching for you, and I believe in you Onslo - and your plan.

The geese and ducks waited all afternoon, not moving from where Onslo placed them on the ice. The shadows lengthened and the sun moved low in the sky. It was about to get dark, too dark for Onslo's plan to work. Onslo could feel his wing tips get nervous again. Everyone was quiet - especially Nick, who seemed deep in thought.

It was then that Nick looked over to Onslo and said calmly, "Onslo, thanks to you I'm not worrying any more. I know your dad will come back for you, and when he does he'll rescue us. I see now that you were right to read and talk to ducks. I'm sorry I made fun of you."

"nn .. Yeh!" said Norman. "I believe you too...but I still don't know what's goin' on."

Just then, Onslo saw a familiar shape in the dusk, a solitary goose soaring high above the far tree line. The flying goose looked in every direction and this is what he saw many feet below: hundreds of ducks lined up on the icy part of a small lake, their bodies spelling out a message:

Seconds later Onslo's father swooped down and landed on the lake,
calling Onslo's name and crying goose tears of joy.
They were rescued.

Love kept its promise.

Onslo's father flew back to find the flock of geese and brought them all back to where Onslo, Nick and Norman were. For two weeks, they stayed until all could fly. And now every year the flock stops at Leg Lake to visit the Merganzers and the other ducks, swans and all their friends near Cathead Bay.

Made in the USA
Columbia, SC
22 October 2018